Crow Chief

Also by Paul Goble:

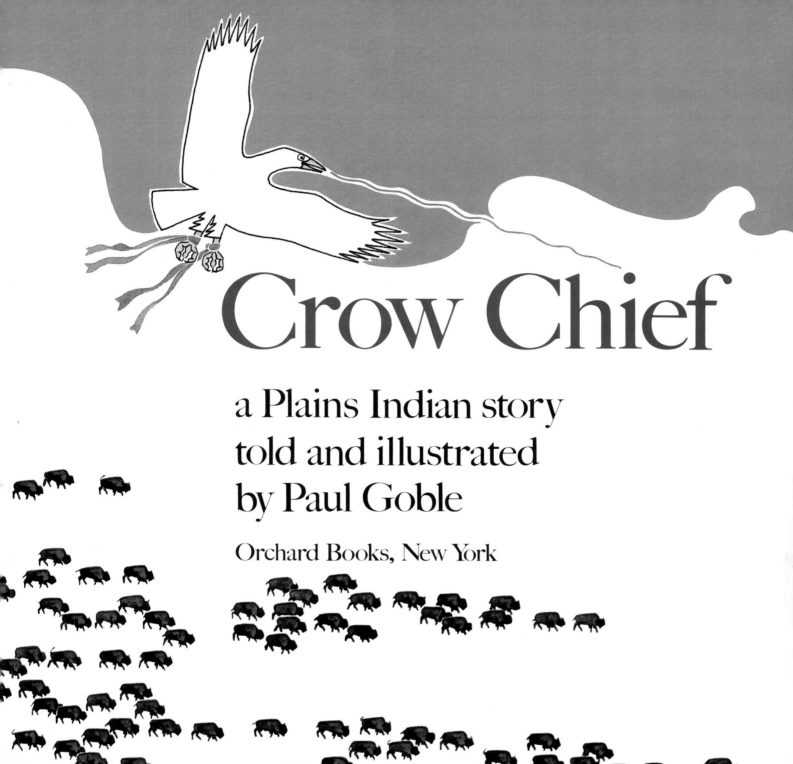

Crow Chief

a Plains Indian story
told and illustrated
by Paul Goble

Orchard Books, New York

for Janet and Robert, with all my love

References

Maurice Boyd, *Kiowa Voices,* Texas Christian University Press, Fort Worth, 1983. George A. Dorsey and Alfred L. Kroeber, *Traditions of the Arapaho,* Field Museum of Natural History, Anthropological Papers V, Chicago, 1903. Richard Erdoes, *The Sound of Flutes,* Pantheon Books, New York, 1976. George Bird Grinnell, *By Cheyenne Campfires,* Yale University Press, New Haven, 1926. James LaPointe, *Legends of the Lakota,* Indian Historian Press, San Francisco, 1976. John G. Neihardt, *Eagle Voice,* Andrew Melrose, London, 1953. Vivian One Feather, *Ehanni Ohunkakan,* Red Cloud Indian School, Pine Ridge, 1974. Ronald Theisz, *Buckskin Tokens,* North Plains Press, Aberdeen, 1975. Clark Wissler and D. C. Duvall, *Mythology of the Blackfoot Indians,* Anthropological Papers of the American Museum of Natural History, New York, 1909.

A Note about the Story

This story relates one of the many wonderful triumphs of Falling Star, the Savior. He is known to different peoples by such names as Stone Boy, Blood Clot Boy, Lodge Boy, or White Plume Boy. Henry Wadsworth Longfellow captured the spirit of similar achievements of an unspecified Iroquois or Ojibwa Savior in his familiar "Song of Hiawatha." The myths vary, but they all speak of the Savior's miraculous birth and his wisdom even as a little boy. He embodies the ideals of bravery, wisdom, kindness, and generosity. He never ages, and travels ceaselessly to help bring order to chaos, and right to wrong.

The story is far older than the coming of horses to the Great Plains, when hunting buffalo became much easier. It dates from the time when it was often difficult to kill buffalo in sufficient numbers so that everyone had enough meat during the winter months. People could not stalk the herds on the treeless plains. Instead, they killed them by a combination of skillful enticement and slow driving of herds over cliffs, through gullies, into pounds or box canyons—anywhere they could be killed easily. Many such sites are known on the plains. It was dangerous and difficult work; it could take many days, and required everyone knowing exactly what to do. Even a dog barking, a child playing, or a crow calling at the wrong moment could cause the herds to shy away, leaving people without meat, and hungry.

Much depended upon the knowledge and skill, and the sacred power, of the man who led the hunt, the "buffalo caller" as he was known. He is a powerful and truly mysterious figure in ancient Plains Indian life. Disguised as a buffalo, he would leave camp, usually for several days, patiently to draw the buffalo herds into the traps where everyone waited to kill them. He had developed a special relationship with the buffalo; he could lead them because he loved them, and understood their thoughts and fears and curiosities.

One speculates that there had to be some "explanation" for times of famine, when the buffalo caller was unsuccessful and the vast herds of buffalo would not be driven into the pounds. Perhaps the herds were simply nowhere to be found in the vicinity of the camp. At such times it must surely have seemed that even the very crows were in league with the buffalo against the hunters. Telling a story like *Crow Chief* perhaps helped both to "explain" the failure of the hunt and to turn away the terrors of famine. It was not a tale just to entertain children.

The story dates from the ancient times when Indian people hunted buffalo because that was their main food. Hunting was work. People killed only what they needed. They had no concept of today's hunting for "sport." They were in harmony with everything in nature, and had lived so for many thousands of years. They hunted as did the hawks and mountain lions, like the snakes and spiders. It was as the Creator intended. It was truly the Golden Age for Indian people.

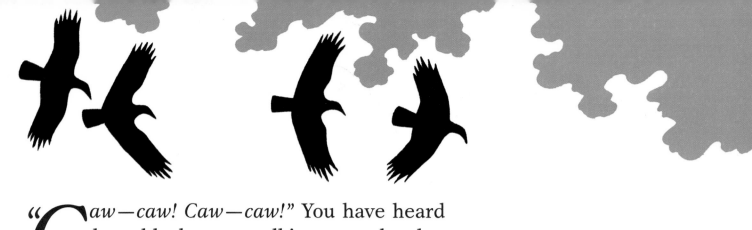

"Caw—caw! Caw—caw!" You have heard those black crows talking to each other. Caw—caw! Caw—caw!" all day long.

Did you know that at one time crows were white? Yes. Every member of the *Kanji Oyate*, the Crow Nation, was white. It was long ago, long before people had guns or horses. It was when people hunted buffaloes with stone-headed spears and arrows.

In those long-ago days the Crow Nation once had a great leader. They called him Crow Chief. He hated people because he wanted to be chief over everyone. But he was friends with the buffaloes. Whenever he saw hunters leaving camp, he would fly off, with his followers, and warn the buffaloes: "*Caw—caw—caw!* Hunters are coming! Save yourselves!"

All the buffaloes would run away. The hunters could never get near them, and so they did not bring home any meat. Nobody had enough to eat.

If a buffalo was too slow, Crow Chief would fly down and land on its back and peck angrily: *"Caw! Caw! Caw!* Did you hear what I said? HUNTERS ARE COMING! They will kill you! They will drink your blood! They will eat your kidneys! They will cut up your flesh, slice by slice, and dry it in the sun! They will use your shaggy robe to keep themselves warm in winter! HURRY!"

The hunters could never get near the buffaloes. Day after day they returned empty-handed. Children cried with hunger, but their mothers did not have any meat to give them. They prayed for help.

Their prayers were answered: a young man called Falling Star came to the camp. He is always traveling from one place to another to rescue people who are in trouble. He listened to their story, and promised to help.

"Bring me a buffalo robe which has the horns and hoofs attached to it," Falling Star told the people. "Pitch a tipi at the center of the camp circle, and paint buffaloes on the outside. Tomorrow morning, let the hunters go out, just as usual."

When the sun was setting, Falling Star told the people: "Go to your tipis now. Put out your fires, close the smoke flaps, tie down your doors, and keep silence. Mothers, do not even let your babies cry."

Falling Star chose a young man to go with him, and they shut themselves inside the painted tipi. Soon there were faint sounds of singing, the beat of a drum, rattles shaking. They were talking to the buffalo spirits.

Early the next morning Falling Star and the young man walked out of the tipi. They were hidden underneath the robe, pretending to be a buffalo bull.

Crow Chief was still half-asleep. He thought it was just an aged bull who had wandered off during the night and was plodding back to join the herd.

Crow Chief watched the hunters sharpening their knives and stringing their bows. When they left camp, he flew off, as he always did, to warn the buffaloes: "*Caw—caw!* Hunters are coming!"

The herd started to run, and soon the sound of their hoofs was like thunder as they stampeded away.

Not the old bull....He fell further and further behind. "Are you deaf, you decrepit old bull?" Crow Chief screamed. "RUN! If the hunters don't get you, the wolves soon will. *Caw—caw!* HURRY!"

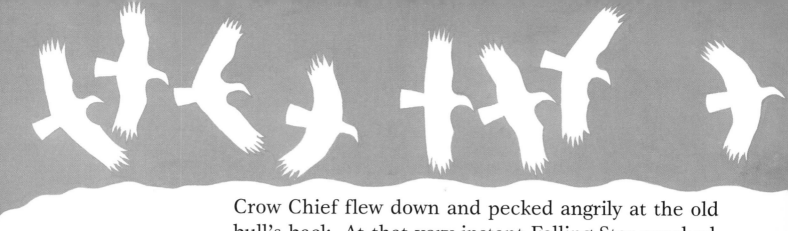

Crow Chief flew down and pecked angrily at the old bull's back. At that very instant Falling Star reached up and caught Crow Chief by his legs! Yes! That wicked bird was a prisoner! At last!

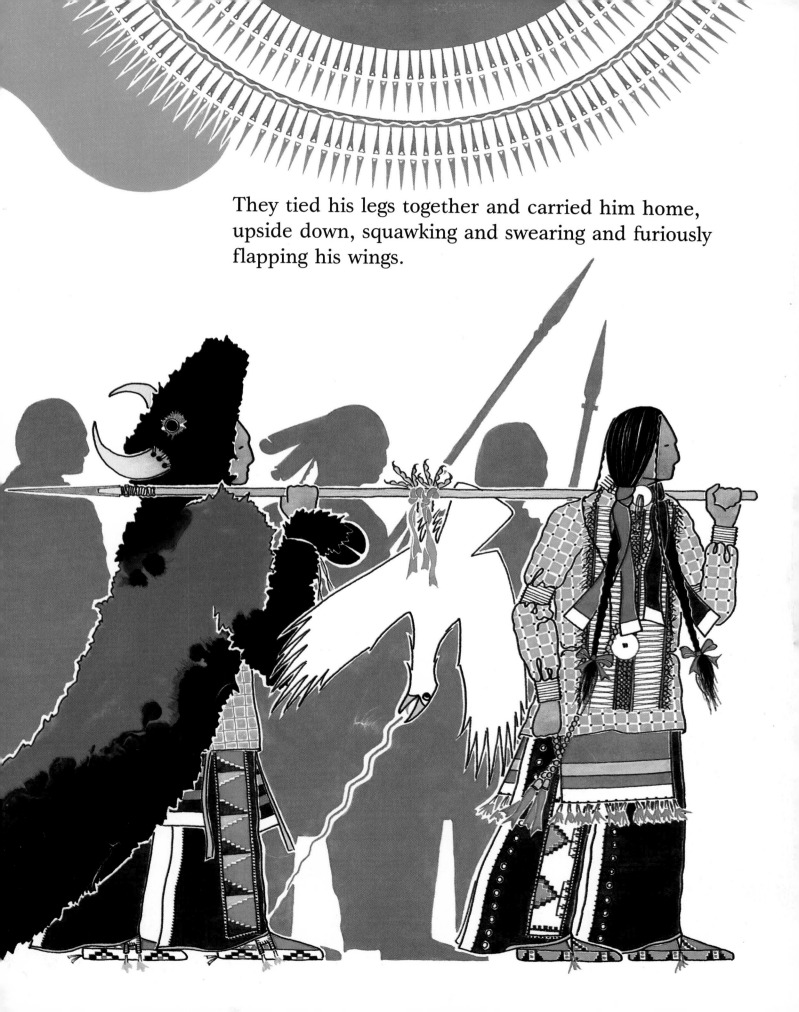

They tied his legs together and carried him home,
upside down, squawking and swearing and furiously
flapping his wings.

Everyone gathered to decide what to do with the prisoner.

"Kill him! Kill him!" people shouted.

"Put his eyes out!" someone screamed.

"Split his tongue!" shouted another.

"No…" Falling Star said. "We will tie him to the tipi poles. He will watch us feasting, and feel the pain of hunger."

After that the hunters brought home all the meat they could carry. Cooking fires were burning all day long. Everyone was happy. Everyone feasted.

But not Crow Chief....He was tied where the tipi poles cross together. He had to sit in the smoke and the delicious aroma of the cooking fire down below. They kept him a prisoner until his feathers were black with soot.

"Have pity on me! *Onshimala ye!* Have pity on me!" he cried again and again.

One day Falling Star untied his legs and said: "The Creator told us to share and live like relatives together. Do not forget again. From now on your people will always be black feathered, as a reminder. Go!"

Crows have been black ever since. They never forget.
They are still talking about it. Every mother crow
tells the story to her young ones. It is true.

After that they followed behind the hunters to eat
the pieces of meat which the hunters left for them.
Everyone got enough to eat. There was peace.

Falling Star still travels from one place to another
to help people. One day, when we need him, he will
come again.

"*Caw—caw! Caw—caw!*" You have heard
those black crows talking to each other.
"*Caw—caw! Caw—caw!*" all day long.

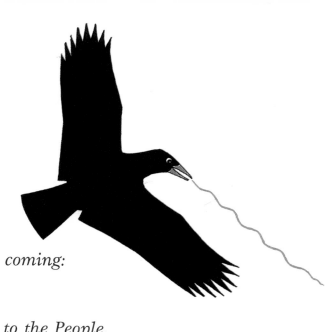

Old Songs about the Crow:

From all over the earth they are coming:
A Nation is coming!
A Nation is coming!
The Eagle has brought the news to the People.

From over the whole earth they are coming:
The Buffaloes are coming!
The Buffaloes are coming!
The Crow has brought the news to the People.
        (Lakota)

The Crow circles above me.
The Crow circles above me.
He has come to take me up.
        (Arapaho)

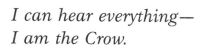

I can hear everything—
I am the Crow.
        (Arapaho)

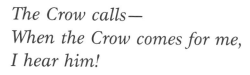

The Crow calls—
When the Crow comes for me,
I hear him!
        (Arapaho)